A Firm Determination to Do or Die

The Defense and Fall of the Peach Orchard Salient
at Gettysburg, July 2, 1863

by
Gary Schreckengost

PublishAmerica
Baltimore

ISBN: 978-1-61546-940-6
PUBLISHED BY PUBLISHAMERICA, LLLP
www.publishamerica.com
Baltimore

Printed in the United States of America

Dedication

Dedicated to the next generation of young readers; to know thy history is to know thyself.

Preface

The battle of Gettysburg was a turning point in the Civil War if not *the* turning point not because the Federal Army of the Potomac won the battle, but because it simply did not lose; because General Robert E. Lee, commander of the famous Confederate Army of Northern Virginia, did not win. Make no mistake about it, Lee went north into Pennsylvania to destroy President Lincoln's main army of operations, the Army of the Potomac, and then swing south to surround Washington, D.C., the Federal capital, hoping it would lead to a negotiated settlement that finally recognized Southern independence from the United States.

In this, Lee came close.

I have created a historically accurate yet fictitious character around John Tricker, an actual member of the famous 114th Pennsylvania Volunteer Infantry Regiment (Collis's Philadelphia Zouaves) to help tell a small but significant part of the story of this fateful campaign. The Philadelphia Zouaves, along with several other Federal regiments, held the very center of the Union line at Gettysburg on July 2, 1863, at a place that we now famously call "The Peach Orchard." Although John Tricker and his brother, Alfred, were actual members of Company B, 114th Pennsylvania, I know little to nothing about them. I don't think anyone today does. I have simply combined my historical knowledge with my own combat experiences in Fallujah, Iraq, as an Iraqi Army advisor from 2005-06, to try to bring the desperate fight for the Peach Orchard Salient more to life for the average reader by using Sergeant John Tricker as a vehicle. I hope you enjoy the book and are inspired to read more about the Gettysburg Campaign and the Civil War in general.

Gary Schreckengost
Lancaster County, PA, June 2009
http://schreckbooks.blogspot.com/
pzrschreck@dejazzd.com

Chapter 1
War!

On December 20, 1860, in the wake of Abraham Lincoln's election as President of the United States, South Carolina seceded from the Union and declared itself an independent country. By February 1861, six other Southern states—Mississippi, Florida, Alabama, Georgia, Louisiana, and Texas—followed South Carolina's lead and on February 8, 1861, adjoined to form the "Confederate States of America."

At the time, I was 25 years old and I and my younger brother, Alfred Tricker, were living on the second floor of my mother's house at the corner of Third and Vine streets just south of Frankford Federal Arsenal in Philadelphia. Having an education, we worked as clerks with a major shipping company that was down along the Delaware River at the foot of Spring Garden Street. It was a good job, I guess. Our father, who had died a few years before, worked there, too.

Alfred and I were also members of the National Grays, a standing Pennsylvania militia organization that had a private armory near the arsenal. It was basically a gentlemen's club in which members had to be voted in by the others. There we drank, played cards, smoked cigars, and generally went hog wild as that sort of behavior was not accepted at home. What set us apart from other gentlemen clubs in the area, however, was that we were a military club. For instance, before we reveled, we would, with our grey uniforms with black trim and big black leather shakos, practice military drill with old muskets or wooden facsimiles. At times, we'd practice with other military clubs, like the Washington Grays, who also drilled on old artillery pieces down along the Delaware River.

Other standing militia organizations in the city included the Philadelphia City Cavalry, which dated itself back to 1774, the National Guards, which had a wonderful armory on Fifth and Race Street, not far from my house, the

Philadelphia Light Guards who had an armory up Chestnut Street past Independence Hall, General Robert Patterson's Scott Legion on Locust Street, the Washington Blues, the National, Philadelphia, Cadwalader, West Philadelphia, and Independent Grays, the Hibernia Greens, the State Fencibles, and the Lafayette, Washington, Sarsfield, Philadelphia, and Jackson rifles.

All of these units, which varied in size, were recognized as being the heart of the Pennsylvania Militia. In time of local emergency, we would be called up by the governor to help support the Philadelphia police in putting down riots and such, like we did during the 1840s. Alfred and I, of course, were too young at the time, but the older fellers told us all about the Anti-Catholic riots that swept the city. In a time of war, we would be called up to form the base company of a volunteer infantry regiment that would be federalized for at least three month's active duty (the president could, without Congressional support, call up volunteers for three month's federal service). None of this service, as of yet, was obligatory, and as such, many Pennsylvanians, who were pacifists opposed to war, were alright with it.

Generally, a volunteer infantry regiment, like in the regular army, would consist of ten-100-man companies, commanded by an elected colonel, lieutenant colonel, and major. Each company was commanded by an elected captain, a couple lieutenants, and several sergeants and corporals. We were told that if the federal government ever mobilized us for war, the men of our organization, the National Grays, would become the seeds of the new companies acting as their captains, lieutenants, and sergeants. The ten elected captains would then get together to elect the regiment's field grade officers, the colonel, lieutenant colonel, and the major. The captain who got the most votes would become the colonel, the second-most the lieutenant colonel, and the third-most would become the major. But in some organizations, like the National Grays, we already had elected field grades because we were already divided into small companies.

Clear as mud? Good.

Philadelphia was always known to be a Democratic town. We tended to favor Southern interests; at least the merchant classes did, although we did have a strong streak of liberal Republicanism in us, too, especially among the Quakers, who still held a lot of power in the city. Needless to say, the city went for the Democrat Steven Douglas for president in 1860 and not Abraham Lincoln. We didn't vote for the National or "Southern" Democrat, John

Breckinridge, either. As for me, I voted for Steven Douglas because I thought that both Lincoln and Breckinridge were too radical to get my vote.

When South Carolina and the rest of the lower South seceded from the United States after the election, however, I was furious. I did not understand their purpose. It got even angrier during the winter, while James Buchanan was still president, when I learned that his Secretary of War, John B. Floyd, had secretly moved all the good weapons from the Frankford Arsenal down to Virginia to get them closer to rebel hands. Then I heard that regular army troops in Texas were being held as hostages by rebels—an act of war. Then the U.S. revenue cutters *William Aiken* and *Dodge* were seized by the Southern Confederacy—another act of war. Then the S.S. *Star of the West*, sent to supply Federal soldiers in Charleston Harbor, South Carolina, was fired upon—yet another act of war—and almost all U.S. offices, mints, forts, naval yards, or arsenals within the Confederacy's proclaimed borders, such as Forts Moultrie, Pinkney, and Johnson in South Carolina, Forts Pulaski and Jackson in Georgia, Forts Morgan and Gaines in Alabama, Forts Marion and Barrancas in Florida, and Forts Jackson, Philip, Pike, and McComb in Louisiana had been seized by the rebel government by force of arms. Only Fort Sumter, in South Carolina, and Forts Pickens and Taylor in Florida remained in U.S. hands.

On Tuesday, March 5, 1861, I learned more about our new president after I read his inaugural address to the nation. What impressed me the most was his conservative stand on the slavery issue, his willingness to seek peace, and his stalwart defense of the country. I was especially drawn two his closing statement:

In *your* hands, my dissatisfied fellow-countrymen, and not in *mine,* is the momentous issue of civil war. The Government will not assail *you.* You can have no conflict without being yourselves the aggressors. *You* have no oath registered in heaven to destroy the Government, while I shall have the most solemn one to "preserve, protect, and defend it." We are not enemies, but friends. We must not be enemies. Though passion may have strained it must not break our bonds of affection. The mystic chords of memory, stretching from every battlefield and patriot grave to every living heart and hearthstone all over this broad land, will yet swell the chorus of the Union, when again touched, as surely they will be, by the better angels of our nature.

That speech cinched it for me and the other members of the National Grays.

Although most of us were Democrats by party, we were Americans by country and as voluntary members of the Pennsylvania Militia, we had already sworn to protect and defend the Constitutions of the Commonwealth of Pennsylvania and the United States of America against "all enemies, foreign or domestic." That didn't mean that we suddenly loved Lincoln, for we did not. We were against his pro-tariff position, as we favored free trade, and we were against his taxation policies for "internal improvements" as we thought they were state or private industry issues, and not the role of the national government as per Article 1, Section 8, Clauses 1-18. He was simply our legally elected president and, in 1864, we would work to unelect him.

Things seemed quiet, but on edge, for the rest of March, which was colder-than-normal here in Philadelphia, getting blanketed with two storms of "onion snow." Onion snow is what we Pennsylvanians call an early-spring wet snow. Usually it comes and goes, but this year, it stayed. Everything changed on April 12 when the rebels attacked and took Fort Sumter, South Carolina. We were totally outraged by this blatant act of Southern rebel aggression.

On April 15, two days after attack, President Lincoln called up for three-months' service "the militia of the several States of the Union, to the aggregate number of 75,000, in order to suppress the rebellion and to maintain the honor, the integrity, and the existence of our national Union, and the perpetuity of popular government, and to redress the wrongs already long enough endured. I deem it proper to say that the first service assigned to the forces hereby called forth, will probably be to re-possess the forts, places, and property which have been seized from the Union." The reasons for Lincoln's limited call were two fold. First, the president was constitutionally limited to call up only 75,000 for three-month's service without Congressional approval. When he took office, Congress was not in session and would not be until early summer. Only then could he request more men for a longer term of service. Secondly, he did not want to alienate the Upper South, those slave states that were still loyal to the United States such as Maryland, Delaware, Virginia, North Carolina, Kentucky, Tennessee, Missouri, and Arkansas.

Well, that didn't work. Refusing to raise its hand against its sister slave states, Maryland, Kentucky, Missouri, Arkansas, and Tennessee refused to heed Lincoln's call and Virginia, the Old Dominion State, outright left the Union and threw in its lot with the Confederacy. Before long, North Carolina, Tennessee, and Arkansas also seceded and Maryland and Missouri were threatening to do so.

The city went ape and all militiamen were asked to rally at their armories to prepare to take in new recruits. Although Alfred and I knew that there was a chance of war, we really didn't think it would come to this. Would our gentlemen's club, that had played war over the past, really be able to conduct war?

With that in mind, Alfred and I walked to our armory, in our uniforms, and into the great unknown.

Chapter 2
I Head South as a Three Month Man

On April 24, 1861, Alfred and I were officially mustered into three month's federal service in a yet unnamed company or regiment as we were busily rounding up new recruits for the regiment that we hoped would be commanded by William Lewis, the president of the National Grays and a recognized field grade officer in the Pennsylvania Militia. As we gathered our volunteers, we also drilled on the grounds of Washington Square on Sixth and Walnut streets, just south of Independence Hall. Because of our pre-existing structure, we had little difficulty in drilling or housing the new recruits that fleshed out our organization. The officers were all well-versed in the school of the soldier and were able to bring the men at once under discipline and to impart on them skill in the practice of arms. Alfred and I even looked like old regulars to the new citizen soldiers of the National Grays who still were dressed in the civilian clothes.

The next few weeks were a little unnerving, however, because we in Philadelphia thought that we were best suited and situated to act as the first to rush down to reinforce and save Washington from the rebel Army of Virginia and the rebel hooligans of Baltimore. But because our loyalty to the Lincoln administration was apparently questionable—coming from a staunchly Democratic city—Governor Andrew Curtin, a Republican, held off in officially recognizing our organizations until we filled eight full regiments (eighty companies).

It wasn't until May 4 that our venerable Philadelphia militia organizations were finally mustered into Federal service as the Seventeenth through Twenty-forth Pennsylvania Volunteer Infantry regiments. Can you believe it? Sixteen other regiments from the backwoods of the state were taken in before we were!? I still can't believe it to this day. If we would have been mustered into service when we were ready to go, we would have been to Baltimore in less than a week after the initial call!

I never understood politics in war.

The Washington Grays, the old Pennsylvania Artillery Regiment that we occasionally drilled with, was the first Philadelphia unit to be mustered into Federal service as the 17th Pennsylvania Infantry Regiment. Its selected commander, Francis Patterson, was son of Major General Robert Patterson, the commanding general of the Pennsylvania Militia and the new Federal Department of Pennsylvania.

We of the National Grays were the next, becoming the 18th Pennsylvania Infantry Regiment. Alfred and I were assigned to the regiment's Company B and those who wanted leadership positions were elected by other members of the Grays. Old Peter Fritz was elected our captain, John De Beust as 1st lieutenant, William Schreiber as 2nd lieutenant, Peter Fritz, jr., as 1st sergeant, and Sam Kingsley, William Kain, and James Barret as sergeants. At this point, Alf and I, being relatively new, chose to stay in the ranks.

Captain Fritz said: "John, how come you didn't want to become a sergeant or a corporal?"

"I don't know. We're only in for three months and I'd like to see how it goes. I guess I just don't want the responsibility and besides, I have to take care of my brother."

"Well, you would have gotten paid more and you could have stuck with your brother."

"Maybe so; maybe next time."

"If there is a next time! The war might be over by the time we get down there!"

I didn't think the war would go that quick; I didn't know how long, but not under a year. I mean, look how long it took us to get up and running.

As expected and hoped, William Lewis was elected by the company commanders to be our regimental colonel and Charles Wilhelm and Alexander Newbold became our lieutenant colonel and major, respectively. Thomas Cooper was chosen to be our regimental adjutant. John Gosline, who later commanded the 96th Pennsylvania Infantry Regiment, a Zouave unit, commanded our Company A, and Charles Collis, who would later command the 114th Pennsylvania (the Philadelphia Zouaves), was elected as our sergeant major.

On May 14, the regiment was ordered to move by train to help garrison Fort McHenry, Baltimore, Maryland. It wasn't an exciting job, but considering our level of training and the importance of keeping a lid on the rebel sympathizers in the city, people who had shut down the rail line to Washington a few weeks before, it was a good job. Inside the fort, in fact, were several hundred rebel sympathizers who were being held in the case mates and other parts of the fort, Alfred and I acting as guards.

On June 14, our company and Company K, all under the command of Old Fritzie, marched a long 16 miles to reinforce the guard at the Federal arsenal at Pikesville, Maryland. There we stayed until July 23, two days after the disaster at Bull Run, when we returned to the rest of the regiment at Fort McHenry. On July 29, we were relieved by the quite imposing 5th New York Infantry Regiment (Duryee's Zouaves), were moved into Baltimore by boat, marched to the train station, and reached Philadelphia the next day, mustering out of Federal service on August 7 without even firing a shot or seeing a real rebel like those poor lads at Bull Run.

Chapter 3
I Join Charles Collis's *Zouaves d'Afrique*

Because of the Bull Run defeat, there wasn't much celebration in Philadelphia. There was, however, a bevy of activity. While we were stationed in Baltimore guarding Fort McHenry and the rebel sympathizers, Congress passed and the president signed legislation to raise hundreds of three year volunteer regiments. Of this total, Pennsylvania was expected to raise 94 such regiments, mostly infantry, but also some artillery and cavalry units. And instead of keeping the old regiments in service, 1-25, Pennsylvania decided to start at number 26 and work its way up until it reached 120.

Naturally, some of the recruits for these new battalions came from the old three month units. Most, however, joined only after news of Bull Run and felt that it was their time to step forward.

Each and every one of these men were volunteers.

After we spent a few days at home and at the Grays' arsenal, kicking some back, Alfred and I decided to join one of the new three year regiments. We also decided that since we liked the fancy Zouave uniform of the 5th New York, however, that was the kind of unit we wanted to join. No more cheap militia gray or boring regular army blue!

It didn't take long for us to find such as opportunity because Charles Collis, late of the Washington Grays and the popular sergeant major of 18th Pennsylvania Infantry Regiment, was also so captivated by the men of Duryee's Zouaves that he, with his own money, desired to raise a company of *Zouaves d'Afrique* to act as Major General Nathaniel Banks's personal body guard. Banks was the commanding general of Baltimore during our time at Fort McHenry. In fact, Collis met us in the armory. "Weren't you fellers in the 18th?" Collis asked with a distinct Irish accent.

"Yes, sergeant major, we were."

"Are you looking for a three-year outfit?"

"Yeah, maybe; it depends."

"It depends on what?"

"Zouaves; we like Zouaves," I said.

"Well, my boy, and your name is?"

"John. I'm John Tricker and this is my brother Alfred."

"Well John and Alfred, this is your lucky day! Because, by chance, I am in fact raising a *Zouave* unit and am expecting a shipment of uniforms from France itself! This is great! I've also contracted with Brook's Brothers to get everything else we may need. So can I count on you?"

"Yes. As long as we get those nice Zouave uniforms and get to shoot a reb."

"That will not be a problem, laddy! Not a problem at all!"

And that's how I formally met the famous Charles Collis, a man who would eventually win the Medal of Honor.

On August 17, 1861, we were again mustered into Federal service, this time for three years. And instead of being issued grey uniforms, like the men of the 18th Pennsylvania were, we were issued brand-new French Zouave uniforms that came direct from France. I couldn't believe it!

With our uniform issue, Collis and some of the other men, men who had actually served with the Zouaves, explained to us their significance and the meaning of the exotic uniform. Zouaves (pronounced ZOO-aavs) were originally select units of the French army, which, by 1861, were considered among the elite fighting forces of the world. When France took control of the Arab city of Algiers in 1830, it enlisted the support of a fiercely independent mountain tribe which called itself the *Zouaoua* (pronounced ZWA-wa). These native Zouaves were organized into two battalions under French officers to maintain order among the Arab population. By 1835 the Zouave battalions evolved to consist of four companies of native Zouaves and two companies of Frenchmen, all uniformed in traditional Zouave dress. By 1841 the native Zouaves were segregated out by government decree to form *Tirailleurs Algeriens* or Turco battalions, and the so-called Zouave battalions thereafter consisted only of Frenchmen. In 1852 three French Zouave regiments of three battalions each were raised; the First Regiment was posted in Blidah, the Second in Oran, and the Third in Constantine.

The French Zouave uniform generally consisted of a red felt fez, a short blue wool jacket, red wool pantaloons, and white canvas leggings. The fez itself, called a *chechia*, was made of red felt and had a dark blue wool tassel attached to its top. The jacket was made of the same dark blue wool as other French uniforms but was cut shorter and made to be worn open. It was trimmed with one-half inch cotton tape that formed an ornate design consisting of a loop leading into a trefoil, which the French called a *tombeau* (pronounced TOM-bow). The color of the tombeau distinguished the Zouave regiments from one another, that is, red for the first, white for the second, and blue for the third. In 1855 a fourth Zouave regiment was raised, drawing the best soldiers from the other three, and it was added to the French Imperial Guard. Both its tassel and tombeau were yellow.

Under the jacket, French Zouaves wore a collarless vest, called a *gilet* (pronounced jeel-A) that was made from a thinner grade of blue wool. It was trimmed around the collar and down the front with the same color *tombeau* as the jacket. Over the vest, the Zouaves wore a ten foot long by ten inches wide light blue sash, called a *ceinture*, that essentially served three purposes: to help carry heavy packs, to act as a wrap around during cold desert nights, and to help support their distinctive loose fitting pantaloons, called *serouel*, which were made of dark red wool. The *serouel* was tucked into white canvas leggings which were fastened with buttons. To help hold the leggings up, the Zouaves would often strap on a pair of leather grieves, called *jambières* (pronounced Zhawm-bee-AIR), just below the knees.

French Zouaves were trained primarily in light infantry tactics collectively referred to as *Chasseur á Pied*. Proponents of this tactic believed that, with the increased range and use of the rifle musket, battlefield success could only be achieved through quick maneuver, malleable formations, and aggressive action. Zouaves were thus taught to begin engaging targets at about three hundred yards, load while they advanced fifty yards at a time at the double quick, kneel, aim, and fire again. They were to do this until they reached about one hundred yards from the opposing line where they were to fire their last volley, concentrate, charge, and smash the enemy with their expert use of the bayonet. The salient points of *Chasseur à Pied*, then, were rapid movement and aggressive action rather than simply standing still one hundred yards from the enemy and exchanging volleys. Maneuver, fire, and charge decisively: these, as in the days of the Roman Legions, were the keys to victory.

During the Crimean War (1854-55) and the War for Italian Unification (1858-59), French Zouaves proved themselves to the world by using these aggressive tactics at the battles of Alma, Inkermann, Sebastopol, the Malikoff, Magenta, and Solferino. U.S. Army Captain George McClellan who had been sent by the American government to observe the Crimean War stated in 1855: "Zouaves are the finest light infantry that Europe can produce…the *beau idéal* of a soldier."

Inspired by these gallant warriors, two groups, Colonel Elmer Ellsworth's Zouave Cadets, a Chicago-based militia unit, and an acting troupe, shrewdly calling itself the "Inkermann Zouaves," were formed to show off the French Zouaves' distinctive uniform and drill to American audiences. Touring throughout the country, the genteel style and impressive drill of these sartorial *Zouav d'Afrique* captivated thousands and inspired several standing militia organizations to convert over to the Zouave concept, uniform and all.

Our Zouave uniforms, that of the Philadelphia Zouaves, consisted of brick-red pantaloons, blue jackets with red *tombeau*, a light blue sash, white canvas leggings, and black and brown leather grieves. Without doubt, the uniform was, in my opinion, the sharpest of the entire war on either side. We were trained by 1st Lieutenant Sam Barthoulot and 2nd Lieutenant George Heimat, who served with the French Zouaves and spoke some English, although with a heavy accent. And because Collis liked us, I was appointed a sergeant and Alfred a corporal.

Upon our muster, we were loaded aboard a chartered merchant vessel and sent a few hours down the Delaware River to Fort Delaware, which was positioned on Pea Patch Island right in the middle of the river. The place certainly was not as nice as Fort McHenry (and that wasn't nice), because it was hot and being in the middle of the river, we were constantly swarmed by mosquitoes. In fact, it was so bad, that there were nights that we got hardly any sleep.

To this day I hate mosquitoes and I will never forget the look of my blood squirting out of them when I was able to smash 'em from time to time.

At Fort Delaware we also received our weapons, brand new M1858 Enfield Rifle muskets, not the junk conversion muskets we had with the 18th Pennsylvania, our gear, and the best training in the world from some former French Zouaves, men like 1st Lieutenant Severin Bathoulot,. The M1858 took this massive sword bayonet that was about a foot in length. We all loved it. In fact, we spent more time on bayonet drill than anything else. Of course, we practiced volley fire, but the experienced Zouaves stated that it was *le bayonet* that won the battle. I remember stabbing forward, pulling back to hit someone from behind with the butt of my rifle, then spinning around again. We thrust up, then down, then across. We even turned our muskets about, holding them halfway up the barrel, and thrust them behind us to get an enemy who was hot on our tail. In short, we became very fit and confident soldiers. It was nothing like I every got with the Grays or the old regiment. These men were serious and our company-sized body guard would be a sight to see!

In late September 1861, we finally got our orders to join General Banks's army that was currently headquartered at Harpers Ferry, Virginia. Again taking the steamer *Major Reybold* up the Delaware, we docked at the Arch Street wharf and, as if on parade, marched over to Broad Street, being cheered along the way. It was one of the more memorable events of my life. If that wasn't enough, we were even asked to perform our exquisite musket drill on the grounds of the Academy of Music. After eating our meal, we loaded aboard a train and headed west, toward Harpers Ferry, where we helped guard the headquarters of the U.S. Army of the Shenandoah, General Banks commanding.

Chapter 4
The Long Road to Gettysburg

Over the next several months we stayed close to General Banks's headquarters, acting as his elite guard. It was not a difficult job, but Captain Collis and the lieutenants were sticklers for how we looked. We were fed well and didn't have to roll around in the mud like other units had to. While with Banks, we drove Stonewall Jackson out of the northern stretches of the valley, capturing Winchester in March 1862. In May, we were driven back by Jackson at the battles of Front Royal, Middletown, and Winchester and were sent packing to the north back of the Potomac River at Williamsport.

In June, we drove back into the Shenandoah Valley in conjunction with General Fremont's Mountain Army and General McDowell's Army of the Rappahannock, pushing Jackson back to the southern end. In August, with the defeat of Major General George McClellan's U.S. Army of the Potomac outside of Richmond, Banks's army was reduced to being the 2nd Corps of the newly-minted U.S. Army of Virginia, under Major General John Pope. In this configuration, we once again fought Jackson's horde at the battle of Cedar Mountain, near the railhead at Gordonsville, Virginia.

As the headquarters guard, we took little loss.

At this point, Collis was able to talk the War Department into using his company of now-famous Zouaves (we were in *Harper's Weekly*) to form a new regiment, a Zouave regiment. Because of all the defeats, recruiting was getting difficult and it was felt that a battalion of flashy Zouaves would be the key. The adjutant general and the governor agreed and we were immediately sent to Philadelphia to form a new regiment: the 114th Pennsylvania Volunteer Infantry Regiment (Collis's Zouaves).

To make a long story short, recruiting was not an issue for us, especially once the men started to received their new Brooks Brother-made Zouave uniforms. We assembled at "Camp Banks" in the Northern Liberties, above

Frankford, and Alfred and I were assigned to Company B, commanded by Captain Edward Bowen, who was transferred in from the 75th Pennsylvania to accept a promotion. Our 1st lieutenant was George Schwartz, promoted from sergeant of the *Zouaves d'Afrique*. I was made the company 1st sergeant, a very important job, and Alfred was made our 4th sergeant. All told, we had 103 officers and men in our company, a full complement, half being native-born Americans and the other half being new German or Irish immigrants. Good lads, but sometimes it was hard to understand them.

On September 1, our massive regiment, which numbered over a thousand Zouaves, more than many infantry brigades out on the line, entrained for Washington to get our weapons and equipment. There we were issued either M1860 Springfield Rifle muskets or M1855 British Enfield Rifle muskets, which were longer versions of the M1858. While the Enfield was caliber .577 and the Springfield was caliber .58, we were all issued .577 rounds—which fired just fine out of my Springfield.

There we were assigned to Major General David Birney's 3rd U.S. Corps, a unit that had fought valiantly on the peninsula outside of Richmond in the spring and early summer of 1862, but was now shot-up and in dire need of reinforcement. Interestingly, General Birney was also a one-time member of the Philadelphia militia establishment and he raised the 26th Pennsylvania Volunteer Infantry (Birney's Zouaves), the first three-year regiment from our faire commonwealth.

In September, after the hellacious battle of Antietam, in which we did not participate (thank God), President Lincoln issued his now-famous Emancipation Proclamation. In it, he warned the Southern Confederacy that if they did not stop their rebellion by January 1, 1863, then all slaves in rebel-held territories after that date would be "henceforth and forever free." All those slave owners who were loyal to the United States, however, like those in Delaware, Maryland, Kentucky, and Missouri, could, as per the Constitution, keep them.

This caused an uproar in the ranks with many opinions being shared.

I, for one, was for it and thought for sure that the rebels would take the deal. Others did not believe that the "Confeds" would take the deal and wondered what "henceforth and forever free" actually meant. Henceforth to take our jobs? Marry our women? Others said that Lincoln actually planned to enlist Confederate slaves into the U.S. military to help win the war. All one had to do was to actually read the document. Others believed that "henceforth and forever free" meant shipment to our colony in Liberia, Africa. It was well-known that Lincoln was no starry-eyed abolitionist radical like General Birney, and that he was no friend of the slave or the black man, for that matter.

Nonetheless, some of the more stalwart Democrats in my company, as well as with the rest of the battalion, deserted the army after news of the Emancipation Proclamation came out. Now I can't be sure of their motives—some were cowards—but I can say point blank that I heard several of the men who came to desert complain about Lincoln's new war policy. They'd say things like, "I came to fight for the union and not to free any slave, etc." During this time period, our company lost thirteen Zouaves to desertion: Jacob Bange, Silas Beard, John Cressman, Zach Fowler, Fred Herzog, John Hickey, Sam Hayes, William McFarland, Frank Roberts, Joseph Slange, Gustavus Trone, Sam Wayne, and George Williams.

It was worse than any battle.

After a few more weeks of waiting, General McClellan was relieved as commander of the Army of the Potomac for his failure at not pursuing Lee after Antietam and was replaced by his close confidant Major General Ambrose E. Burnside, "Old Burn." Because Lincoln wanted to put some teeth behind his proclamation to scare the rebels into compliance, he ordered us to attack south and take Richmond as winter began to blow in from the north. It was a horrible time to be out on campaign and we were all surprised and angered by the move, which we saw as being callous.

As we pulled up to Falmouth, on the opposite bank of the Rappahannock River from Fredericksburg in December 1862, we were sent to Franklin's Crossing, below the town. On December 12, the first day of the infamous battle, we were sent in to stop Jackson's counter-attack against the retreating Pennsylvania Reserve Division from the 1st U.S. Corps. Collis, mounted, led our counter-attack, and for this action he was later awarded the Medal of Honor. As a regiment, we lost twelve killed and seventeen wounded. In our company, we lost not a single man.

After a failed flanking march in a late-winter storm a few weeks later, which was later dubbed "the Mud March," Burnside was relieved and replaced by his arch-nemesis Major General "Fighin' Joe" Hooker, commander of the U.S. 1st Corps. Hooker reorganized the army, gave some of us leave, and improved our fighting strength in time for the big spring time push. On May 3, 1863, in the deep woods around Chancellorsville, we took a walloping as our regiment suffered 173 killed and wounded. Of the 27 officers present, only three escaped death or wounds. In our company, we suffered six killed: my brother, Sergeant Alfred Tricker, who fell near me, and Zouaves John Alqueshouse, Albert Holworth, John Springer, Edward Sims, and Sam Whitesell. One man, Zouave Jim Scullen, was wounded. Colonel Collis was so exhausted that he received medical leave and was replaced by Lieutenant Colonel Frederico Cavada. At this point, our company numbered less than fifty men for the next great battle that may have determined the outcome of the entire war: Gettysburg.

Chapter 5
Our March North into Pennsylvania,
June-July 1863

It goes without saying that after the battle of Chancellorsville, with the death of my younger brother, Sergeant Alfred Tricker, I was depressed. We all were. At Chancellorsville, we held all the advantages: superior strength, more fire power, and had even outflanked the Confeds. But somehow, they threw us back over the north side of the river. The only silver lining we saw was the death of Stonewall Jackson. At the time, we did not quite know for sure how it happened; only that it did.

After a few weeks of sitting idle along the north banks of the Rappahannock and Rapidan rivers, we were ordered north to stop a Confederate lunge up the Shenandoah Valley. I figured that the rebels were looking to turn us out of central Virginia and set up a defensive line near Manassas Railroad Junction, the place of two fabled battles. But I was wrong. I learned this when we crossed the Potomac River into Maryland at Leesburg and kept going, up through Frederick, and on to Taneytown, Maryland.

Where is the enemy!? I thought. My God, had they gotten as far north as Pennsylvania!?

Somewhere on the road to Taneytown on the afternoon of June 30, we learned that General Hooker had been replaced by Major General George Gordon Meade, late commander of the 5th Corps. At this point, we really didn't care because we had gone through so many commanders and we were dead tired. As we pulled into bivouac that evening, we all lined up to get paid—finally. The names on this record would go down in history for what we did over the next few days and for us in the 114th Pennsylvania, almost half would be gone from the pay rolls. All told, our regiment, which used to number about a thousand was reduced to 149 Zouaves—a little less than two official companies.

Our brigade, the 1st Brigade, 1st Division, 3rd U.S. Corps, was commanded by Brigadier Charles Graham, one of General Sickles's most trusted brigade commanders. Graham served in the Navy as a midshipman during the War with Mexico. After the war, during the 1850s, he worked as a civilian engineer at the Brooklyn Navy Yard and was, like Sickles, heavily involved in the politics of the entrenched Democratic Party through New York's infamous Tammany Hall. When Congress called for volunteers in 1861, Graham helped raise and then commanded the 74th New York Infantry Regiment, which was part of Congressman Sickles's famed Excelsior (New York) Brigade that became the heart of the 3rd Corps. By Chancellorsville, with Sickles now in command of the corps, Graham was promoted to brigadier general placed at the head of the 1st Brigade, 1st Division, which consisted of six sturdy Pennsylvania regiments, including us Zouaves, where he did a good enough job in leading us during the battle. Not that I'm qualified to make any judgment, but since I was one of his soldiers, that's my opinion.

The battalions of our brigade consisted of the 57th, 63rd, 68th, 105th, 114th, and 141st Pennsylvania Infantry regiments, one of the few all-Pennsylvania brigades in the Army of the Potomac. The 57th Pennsylvania was organized on October 14, 1861, at Camp Curtin, Harrisburg, Pennsylvania, our state's capital. It was commanded by Colonel Peter Sides and numbered 115 officers and men on June 30. The 63rd Pennsylvania was mustered into Federal service at Camp Haus, Washington, D.C., in October 1861. It numbered 246 officers and men before the big battle, was commanded by Major John Danks, and had bulky Austrian Rifle muskets. The 68th Pennsylvania, commanded by Colonel Andrew Tippen, was also known as the "Scott Legion." It was organized around General Patterson's old Philadelphia militia company that trained with the old Grays from time to time. The Scott Legion formed the base element of the three-month 20th Pennsylvania Infantry Regiment, which served in Patterson's Army of Pennsylvania in the northern reaches of the Shenandoah Valley near Harpers Ferry, Virginia, during the first months of the war. After its three months were up, the regiment was disbanded and several of its officers and men, like Tippin, helped organize the 68th Pennsylvania, which was mustered into Federal service at Camp Frankford on September 2, 1862, for three year's service. It was a good unit and of all of the other regiments of the brigade, it was the Scotts who we were the closet. If I didn't like Zouave uniforms so much, I probably would have joined them. They were armed with British Enfield Rifle muskets and numbered 152 officers and men. The 105th

Pennsylvania, also known as the "Wildcat Regiment," was commanded by Colonel Calvin Craig. It was raised from the western mountain counties of the state, thus the term "wild cat," as cougars still inhabited the deep woods. It numbered some 132 men and they were armed with M1861 Springfield Rifle muskets. They were okay, just a little rowdy at times, and were all heavily bearded; looking much like the lumber jacks many of them were before the war. The last battalion of our brigade, the 141st Pennsylvania, was commanded by Colonel Henry Mandill and was from the northern part of the state. It numbered but 149 men and was armed with Springfield or Austrian Rifle muskets.

All told, our brigade had 943 men which, in the beginning of the war, would have numbered a regiment. We were, as one man said, "hanging by our eye lids." The president was having a hard time finding recruits and time was running out. If the rebs beat us here, it was thought, it would probably all be over.

And that we would not allow.

The 3rd Corps, we learned that night, was part of the left wing of the army, led by Major General John Reynolds of the 1st Corps. Our army was in fact advancing in two broad wings, headed for Gettysburg or York and then onto Carlisle or Harrisburg. A cavalry division led each wing and we intended to find the rebs and throw them back, killing, wounding, or capturing as many of them as possible. Reynolds's wing consisted of Brigadier General John Buford's 1st Cavalry Division, the 1st Corps, the 11th Corps, and our very own 3rd Corps, which was in the rear. The other wing was commanded by Major General Henry Slocum of the 12th Corps and it was led by the 2nd Cavalry Division.

Generally, armies liked to march at night, especially in the summer. We'd start about six o'clock in the evening, just as the heat broke, marched for one hour, rested for ten, march another hour, rest for ten, etc., until sunup. At that time, we halted, posted pickets, lit fires, boiled water, and made coffee to soften our hardtack. This concoction we called "shloosh" because that's the sound it made as it went into our stomachs and out the other end a few hours later. Once we ate, we continued marching until around noon, when we went down during the heat of the day, pulling an hour or two of fatigue work, which may have included standing guard. We'd then eat dinner, and at six o'clock or so, do it all over again. In this pattern, we usually covered fifteen miles a day. Other times, we'd just keep marching until we collapsed.

Three Month Men in Philadelphia before they are shipped south or east.
Harper's Weekly

Federal troops fight it out at Chancellorsville.
Harper's Weekly

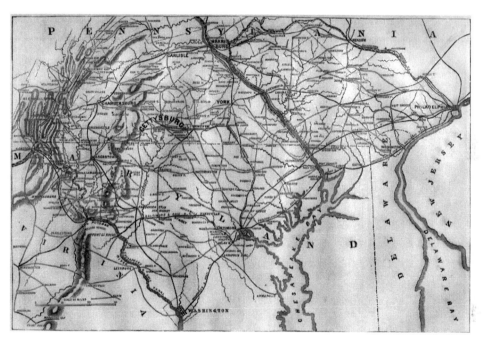

The march to Gettysburg.
Harper's Weekly

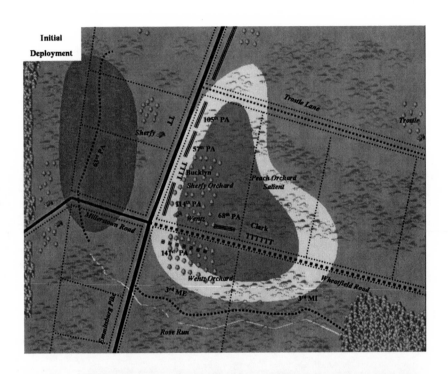

**Initial
Deployment**

Trostle Lane

Trostle

105ᵗʰ PA

Sherfy

57ᵗʰ PA

63ʳᵈ PA

Bucklyn

Sherfy Orchard

Peach Orchard
Salient

114ᵗʰ PA

Wentz

68ᵗʰ PA

Millerstown Road

Clark

141ˢᵗ PA

Wheatfield Road

Wentz Orchard

3ʳᵈ ME

3ʳᵈ MI

Emmitsburg Pike

Rose Run

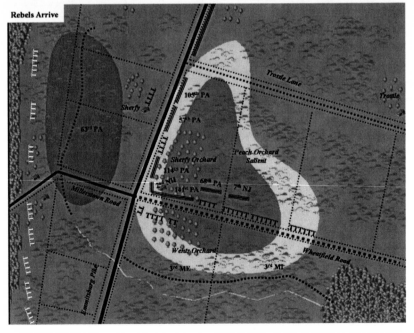

Rebels Arrive

Trostle Lane

Trostle

105ᵗʰ PA

Sherfy

57ᵗʰ PA

63ʳᵈ PA

Sherfy Orchard

Peach Orchard
Salient

114ᵗʰ PA

68ᵗʰ PA

7ᵗʰ NJ

141ˢᵗ PA

Millerstown Road

Wheatfield Road

Wentz Orchard

3ʳᵈ ME

3ʳᵈ MI

Emmitsburg Pike

Position of Lieutenant Samuel McClellan's section, Ames's battery, facing directly west across the Emmitsburg-Gettysburg Pike (foreground). The trees in the background are along Seminary Ridge 700 yards distant where Alexander's Confederate artillery battalion and Barksdale's famed Mississippi infantry brigade were deployed. The tree immediately in front of the gun was not present in 1863.

Author

McClellan's section, Ames's regular army battery, facing west along the pike. The Sherfy barn is in the background to the north and the tree to the right denotes location of the old Wentz house.

Author

Wentz's orchard looking south. Ames's, Hart's, and Thompson's batteries were deployed along the ridge in mid picture, among the trees. The artillery monument in the foreground is erroneously positioned along the Millerstown Road (foreground) for tourists' view only, as the guns were actually positioned about 50 yards forward with an engagement area out past the Rose Farm about 1,500 yards.

Author

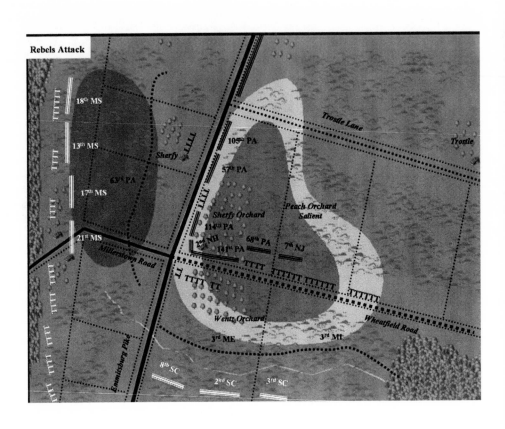

Rebels Attack

18th MS

13th MS

17th MS

63rd PA

21st MS

Millerstown Road

Sherfy

105th PA

57th PA

Trostle Lane

Trostle

Peach Orchard
Salient

Sherfy Orchard

114th PA

2nd NH

141st PA

68th PA

7th NJ

TT

Wentz Orchard

3rd ME

3rd MI

Wheatfield Road

Emmitsburg Pike

8th SC

2nd SC

3rd SC

Looking north up the Emmitsburg Pike toward Gettysburg from the crossroads. Two sections from Bucklyn's Rhode Island battery were deployed in the field to the left, facing left or west, toward Alexander's Confederate artillery battalion, 700 yards distant. To the right of the road were deployed the 114th Pennsylvania, 57th Pennsylvania, and the 105th Pennsylvania. This is where 21st Mississippi Infantry Regiment, Barksdale's infantry brigade, McLaws's division, broke through and rolled up the line.

Author

The view from Little Round Top, looking north toward Cemetery Hill; the Rocky Ridge is to the left and the Peach Orchard Salient is in the left center. The Confederates attacked from left to right, heading for Cemetery Hill from the south and west.

Harper's Weekly

The chaotically brutal fight for the Peach Orchard Salient at Gettysburg, July 2, 1863.
   Battles and Leaders of the Civil War

Atop the Peach Orchard Salient in what used to be Sherfy's Orchard, looking northeast toward Cemetery Ridge and Cemetery Hill, the distant wooded hill on the left. The Trostle farm is just below the ridge behind the monument in mid-picture. This is where Robert E. Lee envisioned Longstreet's artillery to be planted, offering enfilade fire for Powell Hill's Corps, attacking from the left.

Author

Chapter 6
Day 1, July 1, 1863

Soon after midnight, in the very early hours of July 1, 1863, we were drenched by a heavy rain that was complemented by a thunderstorm. Usually, there is nothing worse, in my view, than being soaked to the bone and dead tired. Other than being tired and soaked to the bone, being cold, hungry, tired and soaked to the bone are worse. But because of the heat and the dust, and since we were moving anyway, it didn't bother us too much. What the rain did do, though, was slow us down, as the road, which had already been traversed by the 1st and 11th Corps, was turning into a muddy mire.

At around dawn, as we halted to make breakfast, the rain began to stop. Good soldiers will always keep some dry wood with them, usually in their haversacks. Today was no different. I assumed that this day would be like any other day: that we'd march until noon, rack out, then move on sometime after six.

But today wasn't a normal day as the lead element of our wing, Buford's 1st Cavalry Division, finally came in contact with the enemy north and west of Gettysburg. By nine o'clock, the 1st Corps was engaged and by eleven, the 11th Corps. We were therefore ordered to pick up our pace in the blistering heat with high humidity.

It was sheer torture.

The dampness of the road soon became a curse as the water literally boiled off the surface and ran straight up through our already-sweaty bodies. Before long, we ran out of water and anyone who left the ranks without permission would be shot, by orders of our new commanding general, "Uncle George" Meade. Several men dropped out due to the heat and they were loaded aboard our brigade supply wagons, in the rear of the corps line of march.

By mid-afternoon, as the battle escalated at Gettysburg, throngs of civilians with terror on their faces came down the other side of the road. This slowed us even more, but we had to let them through. They had buggies, cattle, and wagons filled with personal belongings with them. They were of all ages and classes of people, mostly Pennsylvania Germans, who spoke with a strange accent that even we Philadelphia boys didn't quite understand.

We marched into the night up the Emmitsburg-Gettysburg Pike until about 10:00 o'clock, when, in the dark, we were led off the main road, down a farm lane, and into a line of trees, led by some guides. As company-level soldiers, we never knew where we were during these movements, and frankly, it didn't matter. All that did matter was that the temperature was dropping, that we heard crickets and such in the woods that surrounded us, and could begin to smell battle once again. I later found out that we were led east off the Gettysburg Pike, which basically bisected the opposing armies and led straight into Gettysburg, just two miles to our north.

We replaced elements of the 2nd Division, 12th Corps, the famed "White Stars." They were called the White Stars because the 12th Corps's symbol was a star and its second division was white. This held true for the entire army as each corps, the 1st, 2nd, 5th, 6th, 11th, and 12th all had symbols. Each division in a corps then had different colors: red for the first division, white for the second, and blue for the third. Our symbol was a red diamond, for the 1st Division, 3rd Corps. Most of us simply cut out square pieces of red wool and angled it to look like a diamond. While most of the regular units, those with kepis, sewed the colored patches on the soft right front of their kepis, we Philadelphia Zouaves, the only Zouave unit in the entire 1st Division, 3rd Corps, didn't sew on a patch. Well, most of us, anyway. I didn't. Those who did sewed their patch inside the right trefoil of our Zouave jacket.

After replacing the White Stars, I remember being positioned along a low stone farm wall in front of a farm field in the middle of the night and Captain Bowen telling us that the rebs were to our west, the direction from which we marched, that the 2nd Division, 3rd Corps, was to our right, and the 2nd and 3rd brigades, 1st Division, 3rd Corps were to our left, on Little Round Top. Past that was the cavalry. It wasn't a bad spot—it was dark, and I heard no firing at the time. I was just happy to be where I was with Corporal Charles Gentry of my old neighborhood. Along this wall, from around midnight until the late-morning of July 2, 1863, my brigade stayed, myself and Corporal Gentry alternating nap times.

It didn't last long.

Chapter 7
We Move into the Peach Orchard Salient,
July 2, 1863

As the sun came up on July 2, 1863, I noticed that the field to my front was in fact pretty small and there was a farm, what I later learned was owned by George Weikert, out past some trees. Further in front of us, on some high ground, was the Emmitsburg-Gettysburg Pike, the route that Reynolds's left wing had taken to Gettysburg the day before. In short, the battle did not go well for us on July 1, as we were driven back through the town with heavy casualties, barely holding at Cemetery Hill, which was to our right, about two miles away. General Reynolds himself was killed.

At around 8:00 o'clock, I was chosen to act as one of the brigade scouts that were sent forward to reinforce the green-clad 1st U.S. Sharpshooters who were out along the fence-lined pike, protecting the army's left wing and our front. While we were armed with single shot rifle muskets, they were armed with Sharps repeaters. I remember hoofing through the field, past Weikert's farm, then through some more tress, across a creek, from which we stopped and filled our canteens with some muddy water, and to an even bigger farm, Trostle's, that was at the bottom of a ridge. This farm had a huge barn; I didn't think they built barns that big. In fact, I never, ever remember seeing anything like it in Virginia and of course in Philadelphia, we didn't have them at all, only warehouses or carriage houses. From Trostle's farm, our detail, led by a captain from the 63rd Pennsylvania, moved up the farm lane, crested the hill, and came upon the fence-lined pike.

From here, we could see everything; and I mean everything. It was, as we all knew at the time, a key piece of ground because behind our right shoulder, about a mile away and down below, was posted General Winfield Scott Hancock's 2nd Corps. Behind our left shoulder, beyond some woods, was Little

Round Top and the rest of the 1st Division, 3rd Corps. If the Confeds ever got artillery on this height, I thought, they'd blow the 2nd Corps away with near flank shots; much like what we suffered from at Chancellorsville and paid dearly for it.

Once we got our bearings, we all strung out along the fence line on the west or far side of the pike. Zouave Abe Groff from my company and I were to the right of a red brick house that I later learned was owned by a Mr. Sherfy. Behind us, across the pike and atop the hill, was a giant peach orchard and another house, this one being smaller than Mr. Sherfy's house. This house was owned by a Mr. Wentz. To the south of Wentz's house was a small dirt road, called the Millerstown Road that crossed the pike east to west. There we sat for several hours, watching and waiting. At about 3:00 o'clock, during the hottest part of the day, we saw the Sharpshooters bounding back from the woods to our front and up thorough the fields. They yelled, "Here come the rebs! Here come the rebs!" Well, here we go, I thought. Groff and I took a harder look into the woods and saw nothing.

Before long, General Sickles and his staff rode up the Sherfy house and surveyed the scene. I saw a lot of pointing and hub-bub and after a few minutes saw several of his staff officers ride back to our main line. The captain of the 63rd Pennsylvania, and I don't remember his name, came down our line and said, "The whole corps is coming forward. Hold your position and watch for the enemy."

I liked that message as I thought we should hold this position, especially since the rebs were in the woods to our front about 500 yards away.

Soon after, I saw my unit, the 1st Brigade, 1st Division, 3rd Corps, march up over the hill from the Trostle farm and into the fields just behind the Peach Orchard, led by the 63rd Pennsylvania. Just before the brigade entered the orchard, Sickles stopped Graham, and pointed in the direction of the crossroads. With that, Graham rode forward through the orchard, spotted us, and yelled, "You men come with me!"

Running up to the Wentz house, we met Graham who said, "Sergeant, we have to hold this position from two directions: from that way, to the west, and that way, to the south. I'm going to bring some guns up here and I need you to help bring the brigade forward."

"No problem, sir! They're in the woods, yonder!"

"Yes, that's what I hear my good man."

"I'm going to put the 63rd Pennsylvania down into that field that you were watching as skirmishers. Behind them will be the 114th Pennsylvania. I want you to put their left on that crossroad. Do you understand!?"

"Yes, sir!" I said when I saluted.

True to his word, the 63rd Pennsylvania, led by the captain of our old skirmish line, crossed the fences and went down into that field, to its bottom, between the pike and the Confederate-held tree line. As they did so, I finally heard the "pop, pop, pop" of Confederate musketry from the woods. Behind them came my Zouave brothers. Running up to Lieutenant Colonel Cavada, who was mounted, I said, "Follow me, sir!" I showed him the crossroads where we were supposed to go, just in front of the Wentz house and between Sherfy's orchard and the pike fence. At first I didn't understand why we were on this side of the road and not the other side, where we could see better. To our right, going north up the pike toward Cemetery Hill, were four guns from Lieutenant John Bucklyn's Battery E, 1st Rhode Island Light Artillery, which had 4.62-inch bronze M1857 Field guns (commonly known as "Napoleons"). To the right of the guns were the 57th Pennsylvania and the 105th Pennsylvania, whose right rested on Trostle Farm Lane. Immediately in front of the 57th Pennsylvania, on the other side of the pike just north of the Sherfy house, were Bucklyn's two remaining guns. They were no doubt to irritate the rebels in the woods and cover the skirmishers, retreating back across the pike and setting up in the field behind Sherfy's orchard. To the right of the 105th Pennsylvania, extending the line out towards the 2nd Corps, were two brigades from Brigadier General Andrew Humphrey's 2nd Division, 3rd Corps. Colonel George Burling's 3rd Infantry Brigade, 2nd Division, 3rd Corps was held in reserve down by the Trostle barn, hidden from view.

Needless to say, we were stretched very thin between the Millerstown Road and Trostle's Lane, so thin, in fact, that were stretched out in a single line, almost like a line of thick skirmishers. To our left, refused, was the 141st Pennsylvania which was on the south side of the Millerstown Road on the high ground in the middle of another peach orchard, Wentz's orchard. And to their left, on the north side of the road, was Captain Judson Clark's Battery B, 1st New Jersey Artillery, which consisted of six 3-inch wrought iron Parrot Rifles. "Three inches" meant that's how big the projectile was in diameter.

Seeing that we were at an angle on high ground in the middle of the battlefield instantly alarmed us. We knew that we would be in a whirlwind soon enough but also felt that if anyone was going to weather this storm, it was going to be Graham's Pennsylvania brigade, led by the famous *Zoauv' d'Afrique.* Hopefully, however, we'd get some more help because as the minutes rolled by we could feel the Confederates in the tree line growing stronger.

Chapter 8
The Bigger Picture

Although I didn't really grasp the bigger picture at the time of the battle, it is important for me to fill in some of the details of what was going on around us. It is true that in the afternoon of July 2, 1863, Major General Daniel Sickles, commander of the 3rd U.S. Corps of Major General George Gordon Meade's Army of the Potomac, President Lincoln's main army of operations, made the unilateral (and controversial) decision of moving his two small divisions from the southern spur of Cemetery Ridge and Little Round Top forward about 1,000 yards to the Rocky Ridge above Devil's Den, the Rose Farm, and the Emmitsburg-Gettysburg Pike, anchored at the now infamous "Peach Orchard," ground that was more dominant than most of what was previously occupied. As I suspected, Sickles apparently determined to deprive the enemy of this decisive terrain—especially George Sherfy's and John Wentz's peach orchards that coursed along the eastern edge of the fenced-in pike for about 800 yards.

This area, now known as "the Peach Orchard" was indeed critical terrain. Not only is it elevated, but more importantly, it also overlooked, flanked, and thus basically dominated the vulnerable part of the Federal line at Gettysburg: Cemetery Ridge, where Major General Winfield Hancock's 2nd Federal Corps was deployed. If the Confederates would have broken through here on July 2 or 3, 1863, the strong Federal position on Cemetery Ridge, but 500 yards beyond, would have been made untenable and the Union army would most likely have been defeated on its own soil, possibly ending the war with Southern independence secured.

In fact, as I later learned, the critical component of Confederate General Robert E. Lee's July 2 battle plan called for the bulk of Lieutenant General James Longstreet's hard-hitting 1st Corps, Army of Northern Virginia, to "attack up the Emmitsburg Pike" from the south, seize the heights of the Peach

Orchard, plant at least two battalions of artillery atop it, suppress Hancock's troops with enfilade fire, continue the *en echelon* infantry attack from the south, breach Hancock's vulnerable line in concert with two divisions from Powell Hill's 3rd Corps coming in from the west, seizing the Taneytown Road and the Baltimore Pike, and surrounding Cemetery Hill, Meade's center of gravity, thus winning the battle if not the war.

In short, the Peach Orchard became the critical piece of ground for the battle of Gettysburg if not the entire war. And there we were, the Philadelphia Zouaves and the rest of Graham's brigade, right in the middle of it, in the eye of the storm.

To our far left, holding the extreme left of the Federal line after Sickles ordered the advance, was Brigadier General Hobart Ward's 2nd Infantry Brigade, Major General David Birney's 1st Division, Major General Daniel Sickles's 3rd Corps, reinforced by one company of light artillery. They were placed on a rocky spur above the Devil's Den about 500 yards west of Little Round Top. It is clear that Sickles did not want the enemy to simply get this position without fighting for it because they could have easily placed a battalion of guns on it and blasted Ward's brigade from Little Round Top. At minimum, Ward would fight from the Rocky Ridge, inflicting heavy Confederate casualties, and then fall back onto Little Round Top. The line then snaked west, forming an "L" around a line of woods behind the Rose farm, in front of what we now call "the Wheatfield." This area was held by Colonel Regis de Trobriand's 3rd Infantry Brigade, 1st Division, 3rd Corps, which was also reinforced by a company of light artillery.

Between the 3rd Infantry Brigade at the Rose farm and us, along the Millerstown Road, was a huge gap, maybe 700 yards wide, which was anchored by Clark's battery on the right and the 110th Pennsylvania Infantry Regiment of de Trobriand's brigade on the left. Aside for being emplaced next to a gaping hole, Clark's battery was in about as perfect as a position as could be found; a gunner's dream with clear fields of fire out to maximum effective range, which was about 1,500 yards.

As you can see, the 3rd Corps, from the Rocky Ridge to the Rose farm to the Peach Orchard, was like a giant "Z" with my brigade holding one of its angles.

To Clark's and the 141st Pennsylvania's front, down the slope and to the south, was a small brook, about 900 yards distant, where the 3rd Maine from

Ward's brigade and the 3rd Michigan from De Trobriand's brigade were deployed as skirmishers. To the right front of the brook, another 200 yards, was George Rose's farmstead, and beyond that, another 500 yards to the southwest, was the Slyder farm. All told, Clark's guns could engage targets, as long as they could be discerned through the haze and smoke of battle, at about 1,500 yards. In other words, Clark could easily engage any approaching Confederate infantry with shell or canister or harangue any Confederate artillery coming into battery within his field of fire with solid shot or shell with devastating effect. His limbers were close—holding at least ten rounds of shot, ten of shell, and five of canister each—and behind them were his extra limbers and caissons, which held quadruple that amount (total of 125 rounds of on-hand ammunition per gun with 25 rounds in each limber chest, including the primary and secondary limbers and three limber chests per each caisson).

Assuming that each gun could fire at least one round per minute, even in the worst of conditions, Clark's guns could conceivably fire 120 rounds of shell or canister in 20 minutes, the time it would take an attacking infantry force to traverse 1,500 yards at the quick and double quick times. And if that attacking force simply assembled in the woods just south of the Slyder house, Clark, who started the battle with 750 total projectiles, would still have 630 rounds left for any bombardment at 1,500 yards range. He'd no doubt fire his 300 rounds of solid first, then his 300 rounds of shell, and then, if needed, his remaining 150 rounds or so of canister at targets under 500 yards range, or in this case, in the middle of the oat field that was to his immediate front. All told, Clark could deliver two hours of sustained fire.

Seeing that we were holding too much ground, Graham went to Sickles, who was in the field behind Sherfy's orchard and asked for more infantry support. Sickles complied and sent up the 2nd New Hampshire and 7th New Jersey from the reserve. Graham placed them to the left of Clark's battery to help fill in the gap—and they did so—stretching out in a thick skirmish line.

Chapter 9
The Confederates Arrive

Soon after the New Hamphiremen and the Jerseys set up near the 141st Pennsylvania and Clark's battery, enemy activity increased across the fields opposite, along the tree line. What we later learned was that Confederate General Robert E. Lee intended to smash the 3rd U.S. Corps and roll up the 2nd Corps, attacking Cemetery Hill, our strong point, from the north, the west, and the south. While Ewell's rebel corps attacked the hill from the north and northeast, Longstreet was to attack from the south up the fence-lined Gettysburg Pike, take the Peach Orchard, move several battalions of artillery on it, overlooking the Trostle farm, fire near enfilade shot and shell into the left of the 2nd Corps, follow up with an infantry assault.

While Longstreet did this, Ambrose Powell Hill's Confederate corps, attacking directly east from the tree line about one mile north of our position, was to attack Hancock's 2nd Corps from the front, throwing it back. Then, at the crescendo of the battle, Longstreet and Hill would attack Cemetery Hill from the south, up the Taneytown Road, and kill, capture, or displace as many Yankees as possible. Once this victory was secured, it was thought, we'd retreat down into Maryland, make another stand, get flanked and beaten again, and then Lee would surround Washington, D.C., holding Lincoln and his government hostage until Southern independence was recognized.

That was the nightmare scenario for us, of course.

Although none of knew exactly what the rebels were up to that day, we all knew that we were going to be in for it when two battalions of Confederate artillery began to emplace just east of the opposing tree line, not 500-800 yards away, and started to open up on Bucklyn's and Clark's guns. Behind them were infantry brigades from Major General La Fayette McLaws's 1st Division, Lieutenant General James Longstreet's 1st Corps, Confederate Army of Northern Virginia. There was no doubt that they were headed straight for us.

McLaws had four brigades of infantry: Brigadier General Joseph Kershaw's brigade from South Carolina, Brigadier General William Barksdale's brigade from Mississippi, and two Georgia brigades under Brigadier Generals Paul Semms and William Wofford. He also had two battalions of artillery with him, Colonel Henry Cabell's, which was to our extreme left front, firing at Clark's battery, and Colonel Edward Porter Alexander's, which was firing on Bucklyn's guns on both sides of the Sherfy house and barn.

Being to the left of Bucklyn's battery, which was masked by the pike (now I understand why we were put on this side of the pike), we caught hell, especially A Company, which was adjoined to the battery. The boys from the 57th and the 105th also caught it, being behind Buckyn's third section of guns north of the house.

Artillery fire is vicious, frightening, and impersonal. It was, by far, the most horrific form of killing on the battlefield because we infantrymen were helpless to stop them. We used to make fun of the artillerists—thinking that they had it easy. On the march, they stowed all their gear on the spare wheels of their limbers or caissons and just walked, carrying no musket or pack; just a canteen. Others rode on the limbers or on the horses at a gentle pace. After the first battle, however, we realized how dangerous their job really was and never said another word. Here was no different.

A company of light artillery generally consisted of three sections of two guns each. A sergeant, called a gunner, commanded each gun, and a lieutenant commanded each section. A captain was in charge of its tactical deployment and a first sergeant dealt with its administrative personnel matters. A company of artillery had the same firepower as a brigade of infantry and each Federal artillery battalion of 30 guns (five batteries of six guns each) had the same firepower as a division of infantry. When a company deployed into a firing line, it was then called a "battery."

The "Number One Man" stood to the right side of the muzzle and the "Number Two Man" stood to the left. As such, these two crewmen were the most exposed men of the section. The "Number Three Man" stood back by the limber chest. He was the "gun bunny." The "Number Four Man" stood on the left side of the gun behind the axle. The "Gunner" straddled the trail of the gun. The "Number Five Man" stood behind the limber chest.

To load and fire a cannon, the gunner would shout out a range and type of round back to the Number Five Man. For example: "Range, 1,800—shell!" The Number Five Man would repeat the command, cut the fuse and prepare the ammunition. As he did so, the Number One Man swabbed the barrel while the "Number Four Man" kept is thumb on the vent hole with a leather thumb-stall to ensure that a vacuum was created in the barrel; so that the powder wouldn't blow up while it was being loaded.

The gun bunny next ran up to the Number Two Man and handed him the ammunition, propellant and fuse. The Number Two Man then inserted the ammunition and the Number One man rammed it home. Once done, the Number One and Two Man stepped away and the gunner, who had balanced his rear sight, called a "Pendulum Hausse" on the gimbals, which were affixed behind the vent, aimed the gun. When he yelled "laid," and pointed his arms in the air, the Number Four Man, the one with the thumb-stall, poked the vent hole with a gunner's tool, stuck in a friction fuse, attached it to his lanyard and waited for the command of "fire!" by the gunner. Once the gun was discharged, it recoiled or jumped back about five yards. The men then wheeled it back into position and the process started again. A good gun crew could fire every thirty seconds.

Each battery contained about 120 men and 100 horses, six horses per limber. The limber towed the gun and carried fifty rounds of rifled ammunition. When a battery took casualties it also lost horses. The reason why there were six horses per gun was for speed and reserve. Only two horses were actually needed. When a horse was killed, it was simply cut away from the team. Three drivers rode the left horses. When in combat, they were responsible for keeping the horses calm, for bringing up the limber up for a hook up, or for replacing the gun crew.

Each section sergeant, the gunner, commanded one gun, one limber, and one caisson with twenty men and twelve horses. The caisson consisted of one limber and one towed caisson that carried two limber chests with 100 rounds of ammunition. It was on the caisson where the men piled their gear, especially on the extra wagon wheel that was mounted on the caisson. That's where the men tied their packs and such instead of carrying them like the infantry.

In the field artillery, there was foot artillery, artillery that was assigned to infantry corps, and horse artillery, or artillery that was assigned to the cavalry corps. In the horse artillery, everyone was mounted. In the foot artillery, however, the only mounted personnel were the drivers (the men who drove the limber or caisson horses), the gunners, and the officers. Everyone else had to walk along side. When a section was ordered "ACTION FRONT!" six of the more nimble or daring cannoneers mounted the three limber chests and hung on for dear life while the drivers galloped forward. This was a dangerous affair, as some of the men were either hurt or killed in the deployment (the ammunition was very fragile and could explode, men could get thrown off, etc). The rest of the gun crew had to run behind. The gun was then dismounted from the limber and put into action.

The artillerists fired three basic types of rounds: shot, shell, and canister. Shot was a solid piece of iron that did not explode. It was either round, bullet-shaped, or was bar shot or chain shot. Bar shot looked like a small dumb bell and chain shot had two iron balls attached with a chain that had devastating effect as it spun into its target. Shell was hallow; it was filled with musket balls and exploded in air or, if no fuse was inserted, acted as solid shot and shattered on impact. It was only good to about 1,500 yards. Apparently, both sides preferred to fill their chests with this versatile round at the expense of solid shot and canister. Canister was a can filled with musket balls and acted as a shotgun blast out to 500 yards.

If crews from Bucklyn's Rhode Island battery went down too far, we Zouaves would be expected to chip in.

Chapter 10
Uncle George Explodes

About an hour after we got finished setting up, and as the Confederates started peppering our position with shot and shell, five more companies of light artillery rolled into our position. I remember the staff officers being extremely agitated and I felt nervous that we were being moved just before a battle. I saw that the 141st was ordered to move when ten pieces of light artillery came tearing across the field to our rear almost at full gallop and were headed for the 141st Pennsylvania's old position in Wentz's orchard. The first guns, Battery G, 1st New York, commanded by Captain Nelson Ames, literally ran a gauntlet of Confederate shot and shell fired from Cabell's battalion, losing two horses. Even worse, Ames's guns were forced to stop at the Millerstown Road to rip down fences, further impeding the battery's advance while under fire.

Wheeling his six Napoleons into Sherfy's orchard and then turning between the rows of neatly planted peach trees about 50 yards south of the Millerstown Road, Ames's gunners had to shift their cannon into position by hand as maneuvering in the orchard itself with six-horse limbers looked extremely difficult from where I was standing at the Wentz house. Once the guns were emplaced, facing south and southwest, the limbers were taken to the southern edge of the Millerstown Road, with the hitches facing south toward the lunettes of each gun. If Ames ordered a retreat, the gunners would have had to pull the guns back by rope or prolonge, hitch them to the limber, then cross the Millerstown Road which was slightly sunken. Unlike Clark's battery, the extra limbers and caissons of Ames's battery were deployed about 200 yards to his left rear, where the ground drops off toward the Trostle Farm in an oat field.

Ames had to have quickly realized that he had been placed in the center of the storm—a crossfire—as he not only began to receive fire from the southwest from Cabell's Confederate artillery battalion, but also deadly enfilade fire from Alexander's battalion to the west. To help counter Alexander's artillerists, Ames judiciously ordered his right section, Lt. Samuel McClellan's, to refuse the line, face west, and engage those guns in conjunction with Bucklyn's guns.

As this occurred, Graham sent the 2nd New Hampshire over to plug the gap between the Zouaves and McClellan's section—right across the Millerstown Road. The reason they were brought over, not only because we needed the help, but because sixteen guns from the army's artillery reserve had come up to fill in that gaping hole, relieving the 2nd New Hampshire and the 7th New Jersey of that yeoman duty. These guns were under the command of Lieutenant Colonel Freeman McGilvery.

The reason for the much-needed artillery reinforcements, we later learned, was because of the commanding general, "Uncle George" Meade. When Meade rode up to discover that Sickles had in fact moved his corps without prior army approval, he exploded on Sickles. We all heard the rumors from the fellers of the headquarters section after the battle, and it was not pretty. Meade, a Philadelphia-born regular army officer, could and would swear up a storm, especially against volunteer officers, especially against politically-connected volunteer officers like Sickles.

It got so bad that Sickles offered to pull us all back to our original positions, which I thought would have been the wrong thing to do. But because the Confederates had already opened their attack against our line, from the Rocky Ridge in the south to the Peach Orchard in the north, Meade decided to support us not only with guns from the army's precious artillery reserve, but also with infantry brigades from the 5th Corps that were just now arriving to the field. So, as the Confederates kicked off their attack soon after 3:00 o'clock, we were finally set with some thirteen battalions of infantry and eight batteries of artillery to face a yet unknown sized element of the enemy.

Chapter 11
Artillery Fight

Over the next hour, from 3:00-4:00 o'clock, Union and Confederate artillery hammered away at each other in a way that both sides later admitted was among the most intense—and most even—during the entire war. Captain Ames, in the very center of the storm, stated that it was as sharp an artillery fight he ever witnessed. Colonel Edward Porter Alexander, Longstreet's nominal artillery chief during the battle and in command of the battalions that faced us on July 2 later remembered, "The range was very close, and the ground we occupied gave little shelter except at a few points for the limbers and caissons. Our losses both of men and horses were the severest the batteries ever suffered in so short a time during the war." Lietenant William Furlong, one of Alexander's battery commanders, reported that that the Federal gunners, "replied with spirit, their fire being incessant, severe, and well-directed."

And although positioned in support, the Federal infantry regiments behind the guns south along the Millerstown Road suffered serious casualties from Confederate counter-battery fire. The staff of the 2nd New Hampshire's flag, for example, was cut in two by shrapnel and several men were cut to pieces by red-hot pieces of razor-sharp artillery shards. Colonel Madill of the 141st Pennsylvania remembered, "Fire from the enemy's artillery fire was very severe and we sustained a considerable loss in killed and wounded." The same held true for the Scott Legion and the 7th New Jersey Infantry who were behind McGilvery's grand battery that was anchored by Clark's New Jersey battery. The guns from Cabell's Confederate battalion, to the south, was really hammering them.

For us, jammed between Bucklyn's Rhode Island battery and the 2nd New Hampshire, and behind the pike that scooted along the ridge top, we were generally protected because if anything, artillery rounds missed long or short and not right or left. I hated artillery because I could do nothing to stop it. Infantry attacks were deemed fair, but artillery attacks were not.

Soon after, Brigadier General Evander M. Law's brigade of Alabamians and Jerome B. Robertson's famous Texas brigade of Hood's division began Lee's famous *en echelon* or progressive attack against the Federal left. But instead of attacking up the Emmitsburg Pike and into the mouths of McGilvery's grand battery along the Millerstown Road, Longstreet correctly directed Hood to attack directly east toward the Rocky Ridge that was held by Ward's 2nd Infantry Brigade, 1st Division, 3rd Corps and Captain James Smith's battery of New York Light.

About a half hour later, the rest of Hood's division attacked. While Brigadier General Henry L. Benning's infantry brigade basically followed Law's attack axis, Brigadier General George "Tige" Anderson's brigade of Georgia infantry steered a little more to the north, crossing the fields just south of the Rose Farm and toward the Wheatfield. For McGilvery's gunners, this was a dream come true as an entire Confederate brigade had exposed its flank to them at a range of less than 1,000 yards. McGilvery therefore ordered some of his guns to continue the counter-battery fight against Cabell while others would fire enfilade shot or shell into or above Anderson's ranks, markedly slowing their progress against De Trobriand's brigade and Captain George Winslow's New York battery which were deployed in the Wheatfield.

At 5:00 P.M., as the sun reached its apex of heat, Confederate Brigadier General Joe Kershaw's South Carolina infantry brigade and Brigadier General Paul Semmes brigade of Georgia infantry, McLaws's 1st Division, passed through Cabell's artillery battalion and launched their attack toward the Wheatfield. These attacking Confederates offered an even more exhilarating target to McKilvery's gunners and Kershaw's brigade was ripped to shreds. In fact, it was too good to be true. The Confederate counter-battery fire was hot, to be true, but generally ineffective as it had only killed or wounded a few of the gunners or the battery horses and did little to nothing in degrading the ability of the batteries to deliver at least one round a minute. Lieutenant Colonel McGilvery reported:

"I immediately trained the entire line of our guns upon them, and opened with various kinds of ammunition. The column continued to move on at double-quick until its head reached a barn and farm-house [Rose's] immediately in front of my left battery, about 450 yards distant, when it came to a halt. I gave them canister and solid shot with such good effect that I am sure that several hundred were put *hors de combat* in a short space of time. The column was broken—part fled in the direction from whence it came; part pushed on into the woods on our left; the remainder endeavored to shelter themselves in masses around the house and barn."

In fact, McGilvery's fire was so intense that Kershaw's left two battalions, those closest to McGilvery's gun line, were stopped cold at the brook, forced to take cover, and ordered by Kershaw to change their front to the north, directly facing Ames's, Thompson's, and Hart's guns. They were ordered to try to kill the gunners with musketry at the insane range of 900 yards. What these two battalions did do, however, were to finally drive the Federal skirmishers from the brook where they then fell back toward the main line, in Wentz's orchard.

The battle was starting to reach a crescendo, and Ames's battery, holding the key position of the line, was beginning to run out of ammunition. As was already stated, its caissons and extra limbers were far to the rear, making resupply almost impossible. Informing Captain George Randolph of his situation, the 3rd U.S. Corps artillery chief dispatched Captain Watkins's Battery I, 5th U.S., recently sent up from the 5th Corps, to replace him. To facilitate the hand over, the 2nd New Hampshire had to yield its position for a time, pulling back north from the road, allowing Ames to move out and Watkins to move in.

Chapter 12
Confederate Infantry Assault

At this point in the battle, although Sickles's far left brigade atop the Rocky Ridge Ridge, Ward's, had been smashed, other elements of the army, namely two 5th Corps brigades and one battery of regular artillery, were holding Little Round Top against what was left of Laws's and Benning's Confederate brigades. The Wheatfield was also still in Federal hands as De Trobriand's 3rd Corps brigade and Winslow's New York battery were systematically being reinforced by eight brigades from the 2nd and 5th Corps. At the Peach Orchard Salient, the key point of the battle, McGilvery's gun line was virtually unassailable, as long as its flanks were secure. And along the Emmitsburg-Gettysburg Pike, the Confederates were yet to attack—that is, until 5:30 P.M.

At 5:30, Brigadier General William Barksdale's hard-hitting Mississippi infantry brigade, about 1,600 strong, followed by Brigadier General William T. Wofford's Georgia brigade, the last of McLaws's division, passed through Alexander's gun line and quickly charged across the fields to our front. Barksdale's line stretched about 800 yards north of the Millerstown Road and Wofford's brigade, about 200 yards behind the Mississippians, was positioned more to the south, the Millerstown Road acting as its center guide.

They were converging on us!

As previously stated, the four guns on the west side of the road, north of the Sherfy farm and in front of the 57th Pennsylvania, were only able to fire off a few rounds of shell and then one of canister before the Mississippians, using the defilade to their advantage, got into their attack position but 200 yards away from the guns where three of Barksdale's four battalions leveled a few deadly volleys uphill into the gun crews. At this point, Captain Randolph, Sickles's artillery chief, rode up to Captain Edward R. Bowen, acting battalion major of our regiment and said: "If you want to save my battery, move forward! I cannot find General Graham! I give the order on my own responsibility. Move the whole line forward!"

Granted, we really didn't want to save that battery, but it was our duty to do so. With the concept in hand, Bowen bolted over what was left of the fence and into the pike to the front of our line and yelled: "BATTALION! Forward! March!" We quickly followed, crossed the pike with a shout, went over, under, or through the opposite fence, and vaulted into the high grass that overlooked the defilade where the attacking rebels were currently attacking our guns. In going over, under, or through the fences, however, our formation became even more disjointed and the Confederates met us with a volley from the declivity. Even worse, we were outnumbered as the 13th and 17th Mississippi were to our front and the 21st Mississippi, coming up astride the Millerstown Road, was approaching our left.

Behind us, the 2nd New Hampshire 3rd Maine, 141st Pennsylvania, and the 3rd Michigan Infantry regiments passed through McGilvery's grand battery, crossed the Wheatfield Road, entered Wentz's orchard, and attacked down the hill against Kershaw's advancing Carolinians. Colonel Bailey of the 2nd New Hampshire later reported:

"My regiment entered the fight with a firm determination to do or die…and advanced 150 yards into the orchard at a run with a yell and such impetuosity as to cause the enemy to retire to a ravine 250 yards in our front, where they were covered from our fire, when I directed the fire of my battalion of the left oblique by the flank at about the same distance. My fire was so galling, assisted by that from the 3rd Maine, which had come up and taken part on my left."

At this point, Graham ordered the Scott Legion to cross the pike to stop the 21st Mississippi and to protect our left flank and the 2nd New Hampshire's right flank. As the 68th Pennsylvania crossed the pike with its proud colors, however, the 21st Mississippi, now deployed behind the western fence along the pike, bushwhacked the Scott Legion at 10-20 yards range, virtually destroying its right wing. Faced with this carnage, Colonel Tippin ordered his men out, and they retreated through Watson's battery behind Clark's, essentially leaving the regular artillerists to their own devices and marking the beginning of the end of the Peach Orchard salient.

Which meant the beginning of the end of us.

And it didn't take long, because once the 21st Mississippi seized the pike, the rest of Graham's brigade was effectively flanked and one by one, the 114th, 57th, and 105th Pennsylvania fell like a row of dominoes. And once the rest of Barksdale's brigade fought its way to the pike, McGilvery's grand battery would also be flanked, his position becoming untenable, especially with elements of Kershaw's and Wofford's brigades pressing its front and right, let alone the guns of Cabell's and Alexander's battalions, which were not only maintaining their bombardment, but were in fact advancing in the wake of the infantry, preparing to hold the Peach Orchard and continue the attack against Cemetery Ridge.

I remember being on the south side of the brown brick house, to the left of it. In front of us were two Confederate battle flags and to our left front was another one, the 21st Mississippi's. The 73rd New York Infantry Regiment of Colonel William Brewster's 2nd Infantry Brigade, Brigadier General Andrew Humphreys' 2nd Division, 3rd Corps, was to our left rear, on the east side of the pike, but at this point, I couldn't see them as I was fully focused to our front. Because Captain Bowen was our acting battalion major, I had to play a stronger role in maneuvering the company.

We fired a few volleys at the advancing Mississippians, who were personally led by their mounted brigadier, Barksdale, who had spooky, long-flowing white hair, looking more like a demon from hell than anything else. To our right, north of the house were the 57th and 105th Pennsylvania and the artillery pieces that were ordered to cover as they retreated from the pike and were headed east, toward the Trostle Farm, to set up our next position.

The volleys made a "Crrackk, crrackk, BOOM!" sound as not all weapons went off at the same time. We Zouaves were in two ranks, the rear rank firing over the right shoulder of the front rank. The Mississippians to our front looked more like a thick skirmish line with each company, like us, firing their own volleys.

With Bucklyn's guns pulled back, we infantry had accomplished our mission and were, no doubt, getting ready to be withdrawn back across the pike to the second fence line to make our next stand when the 21st Mississippi unexpectedly rolled up the Scott Legion, exposing our left flank to murderous enfilade fire. The first companies to go, of course, were those of us on the left, namely mine, which held the extreme left. In fact, the two men who were killed at Gettysburg in our company, Zouaves Abraham Groff and Lewis Borgelt were killed here in quick succession. With the rebels tearing into our flank, my men of course broke to the north and went back through that fence and into the pike. Lieutenant Colonel Cavada and Captain Bowen tried to get us to face south but the fire was too intense and we retreated further up the pike, slamming into the left flank of the 57th Pennsylvania.

It was sheer pandemonium; the worst that I had ever seen during the entire war—even worse than Chancellorsville. I have to admit that I was scared out of my wits and was one of the men who vaulted over the fence and into the temporary safety of Sherfy's orchard. Squatting down with Zouave Charles Gentry of my company, I noticed to the left, at the crossroads, that the 73rd New York was now putting up a staunch defense for a short time until all three Mississippi regiments also converged upon it, seizing the pike, and drove it back. I also noticed through the smoke that most of the infantry units along the Wheatfield Road were pulling back to the top of the hill, behind Sherfy's orchard, and that some of McGilvery's guns were also pulling back.

We were getting surrounded.

Chapter 13
The Fall of the Peach Orchard Salient

At this point, Barksdale's brigade started to form an "L" around the 73rd New York and 57th and 105th Pennsylvania, still in the pike, with the 21st, 17th, and 13th Mississippi coming up from the south and the 18th Mississippi driving in from the west, north of the Sherfy house. During this fight, the 57th and 105th Pennsylvania Infantry regiments lived up to their reputations and fought like wildcats up the pike until they were driven into elements of the 2nd Division, 3rd U.S. Corps.

With the salient essentially blow away at this point, several hundred Confederates in his right rear, and with Graham now reported down and feared captured near the Wentz house, McGilvery ordered the rest of his guns out, starting with Watson's now panicked regulars on the right (they already spiked and abandoned one gun in Wentz's orchard) and cascading left through Clark's New Jersey battery and Phillips's and Bigelow's Massachusetts batteries.

Artillery falling back under pressure of an infantry attack isn't easy. For example, one gun from Phillips's battery had to be pulled out by hand ('by prolonge") and one gun from Thompson's was abandoned due to the loss of its horses; and one battery, Bigelow's, was forced to "retreat by recoil" in order to cover the withdrawal of the rest of the battalion. Retreat by recoil means that the guns, acting as the rear security element, would fire, recoil back about five or so yards and the gun crew, using the backward momentum of the gun, would haul it back a little further, reload, and do it again.

Bigelow's gallant sections, retreating in successive bounds by recoil, firing canister as they went, were aided by Lieutenant Edwin Dow's 6th Maine Battery from Captain Robert Fitzhugh's 4th Volunteer Brigade, Artillery Reserve, just arrived. McGilvery ordered Dow to go into battery midway in the field behind Sherfy's orchard to cover his battalion's withdrawal. It was at this point that Gentry and I decided to get back in the war as we ran forward to offer covering fire for the gunners, trying to inspire other infantrymen from other commands to do the same. Dow's and Bigelow's batteries were under an incessant fire from two batteries of the enemy, situated some 1,000 yards to our front. The gunners replied to them with solid shot and shell until the enemy's line of skirmishers and sharpshooters came out of the woods to the left front of our position and poured a continual stream of bullets at us.

It wasn't good.

Eventually, Charlie and I retreated back into a bowl where the Trostle farm, Sickles's headquarters, was located. At the bottom of it was Bigelow's battery, holding the line, as everyone else had escaped east to Plum Run and where we started the day. To our front left and right was the top of the ridge line, about 300 yards away. Soon, it would be lined with angry Confederate infantry. To my immediate left were some woods. That's where Gentry, myself, and some infantry holdouts decided to make our stand to help cover the left flank of the guns.

The one good thing about a Zouave uniform is that it's easily identifiable from several hundred yards away, even through the din of battle. In this case, Charlie and I acted as a rallying point to the blue trouser infantry. One bad thing about a Zouave uniform is that it's easily identifiable from several hundred yards away, even through the din of battle, as the enemy could spot us, too. Not that we cared, because we wanted everyone to know who we were. But in those woods with the blue trouser boys, I felt my red fez stick out like a sore thumb and chose to take it off and stuff it into my pantaloons.

Bigelow's battery was about to limber up when Colonel McGilvery rode up and said, "Hold your position at all hazards and sacrifice your battery if need be!" Being the last Federal unit on the field, besides my twenty or so men in the woods, Bigelow's battery was all that stood between Longstreet's victorious legions and the now-vacuous Federal center.

Ordering two of his guns out with the rest of what was left of McGilvery's artillery battalion, Bigelow deployed his remaining four Napoleons in a semi-circle and ordered them to fire canister until they were out. It was one of the bravest things I ever saw in my life, especially once the Confederates topped the ridges that overlooked the four guns. In the subsequent contest, all of the battery's horses were killed and Bigelow himself was wounded in the hand.

We tried to cover their left, but the Confederates sent a patrol into the woods and drove us out, too. During our withdrawal, Charlie was wounded in the arm, the final casualty of my small company at the battle of Gettysburg.

Charlie and I hobbled across the bottom lands of Plum Creek and back to the George Weikert farm where we found Lieutenant Colonel Cavada, Captain Bowen, and what was left of the Philadelphia Zouaves. We were a train wreck. After a few more minutes of battle, the Confederates overran Bigelow's brave battery, capturing all of its guns. Their firm determination to do or die enabled reinforcements to come down from the north, however, from the 2nd Corps, and they finally stopped the Confederate attack against our line, especially the brave boys of the 1st Minnesota Infantry Regiment who conducted a desperate charge against an entire Confederate brigade, throwing it back.

Chapter 14
Our Line Buckles but Holds

With the collapse of the Peach Orchard Salient, the entire 3rd Corps line collapsed with it. To the left, Anderson's, Kershaw's, and Semmes's Confederate infantry brigades finally seized the Wheatfield and pushed the Federals all the way back to the northern spur of Little Round Top, only to be stopped by a spoiling attack conducted by two brigades from the Pennsylvania Reserve Division, 5th Corps. And to the right, the brigades of Humphrey's 2nd Division, 3rd Corps, were peeled away from the pike just as Graham's brigade was, but on a larger scale.

With the heights of the Peach Orchard now in rebel hands, just before 7:00 P.M., Confederate Colonel Porter Alexander rushed guns atop it to support Powell Hill's attack, led by Wilcox's infantry brigade, Anderson's division, against Cemetery Ridge, which was currently held by but four brigades from the 2nd Corps (the other six brigades had been sent to help shore up the Federal flanks on Culp's Hill and the Wheatfield).

It was here that the Confederates held victory in their grasp. But for reasons that have yet to be identified, Powell Hill's attack sputtered out like the descending sun on the western horizon, as Mahone's Virginia brigade, Anderson's division, and the four brigades of Pender's crack Light Division were quickly repulsed by Federal artillery fire from Cemetery Ridge and West Cemetery Hill, thus ending Lee's dream of piercing the Federal center and attacking Cemetery Hill from the rear.

In the fight for the Peach Orchard Salient, Graham's Pennsylvania brigade started the fight with 1,516 effectives and suffered 49% casualties with 67 killed, 508 wounded, and 165 missing or captured. Of this, the 141st Pennsylvania suffered the most with a whopping 71% casualty rate (25 killed, 103 wounded, and 21 missing or captured). My unit, the 114th Pennsylvania Infantry Regiment, suffered 9 killed, 46 wounded, and 60 missing out of 259 officers and men (60% loss). The artillery companies of the salient sustained an 18% casualty rate, Bucklyn's Battery E, 1st Rhode Island taking the worst of it with 28% losses (2 killed, 10 wounded, and 1 missing or captured).

As night fell, we knew that our line had buckled, but not broken. The mission was for us to hold the ground around the Weikert farm. In this, we succeeded, inflicting hundreds of casualties on the enemy. Were we thrown back from the salient? Yes. But by making the rebels fight for it—and I'll argue this until the day I die—the rest of the army was able to hold the Plum Run line. There's no doubt we paid a steep price for our fight at the Peach Orchard, suffering 60% casualties, but what would have happened if we would have allowed the Confederates to take the Peach Orchard without a fight and remained along Plum Run? In my opinion, given the ferocity of the rebel attack up hill against us that day, one down hill from the Peach Orchard into the Plum Run line would have probably sent us packing, Longstreet capturing the Taneytown Road to our rear, and cutting off the rest of the army that was dug-in on Cemetery Hill.

The next day, July 3, 1863, Lee made one more grand attempt to dislodge us from our defense, but again we held. We held! Thank goodness for us Philadelphia Zouaves, we only heard the battle rage that day. On July 4, it rained, and a week or so later, what was left of the 3rd Corps, with the rest of the army, pursued the rebels back into Virginia.

General Sickles was horribly wounded during the fight for the Peach Orchard Salient and he was replaced by Major General William French until the corps was disbanded in early 1864. As for us Philadelphia Zouaves, we ended as we began: as a headquarters guard. So reduced by the battles we had fought, especially at Chancellorsville and the Peach Orchard Salient at Gettysburg, we only had a handful left. "Uncle George" Meade, a fellow Philadelphian, therefore decided to make us his headquarters guard until we were mustered out of Federal service in June 1865. The Union was preserved and our constitution was kept in tact and I will never forget the boys in blue who made that happen.

CPSIA information can be obtained at www.ICGtesting.com
Printed in the USA
BVOW05s1058221214

380446BV00001B/179/P